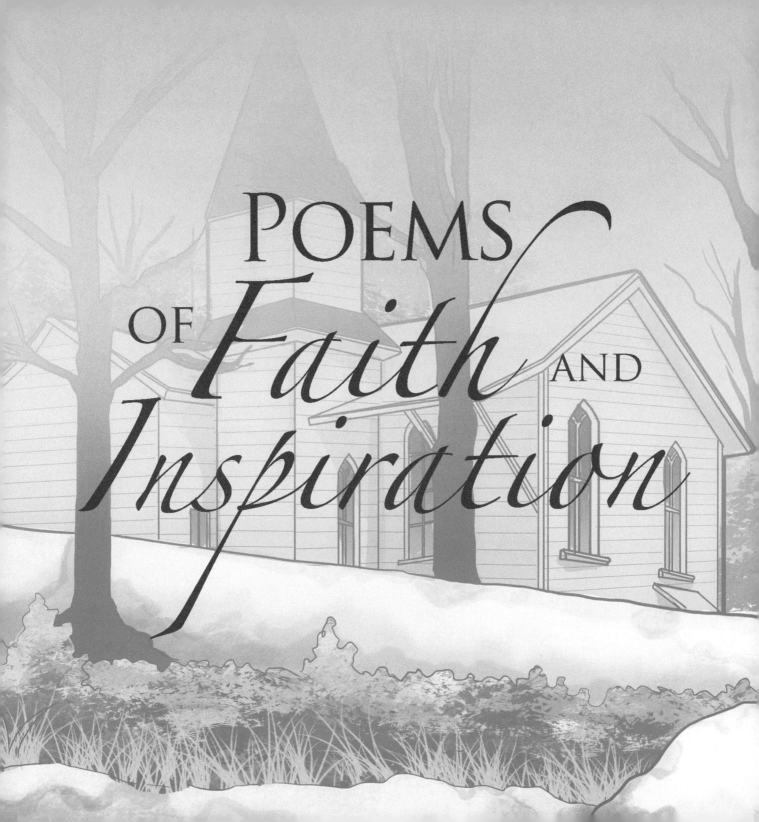

Poems of Faith and Inspiration

Order this book online at www.trafford.com
or email orders@trafford.com

Most Trafford titles are also available at major online book retailers.

Trafford PUBLISHING® www.trafford.com
North America & international
toll-free: 844 688 6899 (USA & Canada)
fax: 812 355 4082

Our mission is to efficiently provide the world's finest, most comprehensive book publishing service, enabling every author to experience success. To find out how to publish your book, your way, and have it available worldwide, visit us online at www.trafford.com

Because of the dynamic nature of the Internet, any web addresses or links contained in this book may have changed since publication and may no longer be valid. The views expressed in this work are solely those of the author and do not necessarily reflect the views of the publisher, and the publisher hereby disclaims any responsibility for them.

Any people depicted in stock imagery provided by Getty Images are models, and such images are being used for illustrative purposes only.
Certain stock imagery © Getty Images.

ISBN: 978-1-6987-1647-3 (sc)
ISBN: 978-1-6987-1648-0 (e)

Library of Congress Control Number: 2024904706

Print information available on the last page.

Trafford rev. 11/22/2024

Contents

Preface 1

Home...3

The Star...4

God's Son 5

The Poor Rich Man 6

Quiet Moments 7

The Promise...9

In the Shadows 10

Turning Point...11

The Vine 12

Great Need 13

The Lamb...14

The Message of the Cross 16

My Cup..17

Loving God 18

Our Prayer 19

Take Heart 20

My Blessing..21

The Shining Lamp 23

God's Touch...24

Peace in the Seasons..26

Blessed Reservation 27

Christmas 29

In Our Place 30

Shepherd Boy and King..31

Memorial Day 32

Hope..33

The Robe..34

Footprints 35

First Easter Morn..36

Noah..37

Giving Thanks 38

God's Gift 39

A Guiding Light 40

These are poems written since the
original ones printed in the book.

Virginia

Preface

It was a beautiful spring day. I was busy going about my daily household chores, and the words "Jesus walked upon the water" kept running through my mind. It was like a record playing over and over. I got my pen and notebook, and I wrote my very first poem, "The Promise."

And so it went over the next four years. I would hear a phrase or a word, and I would be inspired to write another poem.

In John 6:63, Jesus told his followers that human effort accomplishes nothing, but his words are spirit and life. It was then I realized the truth in John 6:63. The truth was for me to write wasn't something I could accomplish by my own effort.

Psalm 68:11 says, "The Lord gave the word, and great are they who proclaim it."

Billy Graham was one of the greatest evangelists of all, a man chosen by God to take the gospel to a lost and sinful world. Billy said, and I quote, "Men and women may devise ways to satisfy their inner longings, but God's way is available in the Bible for all who come to him on his terms."

In John 14:6, Jesus said, "I am the way the truth and the life. No one comes to the father except through me."

That settles it for me. Read God's Word. God speaks to us when we read his word. Read the wonderful story that starts in Genesis and ends in Revelation. It's a glorious wonderful story about what God has done down through the seasons of time. It's the story about the past the present and the future.

I dedicate this book to my beloved family and to my nephew Daniel Ford, who very much inspired me to publish my poems.

In my heart I know that I have been blessed by God to write these poems of faith and inspiration.

Virginia Henderson

Home

Wherever you decide to roam,
Remember the saying, "There is no place like home."
There is the thrill of travel to far off places.
But oh, what joy when we return,
And see our loved ones' familiar happy faces.

Going home to loved ones,
Happy memories come flooding back.
It's like the balm of Gilead
And all the great times we had.

I often wonder about the last great trip
We plan to make.
It will be the greatest trip
We could ever take.

We will be going home
To our home in heaven
And never more to roam,
Then we will know a greater joy
And the true meaning of
No place like home.

Virginia Henderson

The Star

There was a star the shepherds saw.
There was a song the angels sang.
There was a reason why the wise men came.

The star it was so very bright,
Giving out its heavenly light.
The shepherds knew it was a message clear.
It brought a message of the Christ child.
Oh! So very dear.

The angels sang about the Star.
It was to guide the wise men from afar.
Rejoicing, thanking God for leading this night
With a star so beautiful and bright.

The star still shines for some.
For others, the star has never come.
But oh, what joy to believe,
God's grace to receive.

On a night so very long ago,
When God chose to show
His heavenly light
To shepherds far below.

Virginia Henderson

God's Son

He came upon a midnight clear.
He was God's baby son, so very dear.
Angels sang and hovered near.
Mary pressed him close to her breast.
She knew from God she had been blessed.

The wise men came from afar,
Guided by the bright shining star.
They brought precious gifts of gold.
Frankincense and myrrh.
When they gazed upon him,
He didn't even stir.
They knew he was the Holy Child,
It was a scene so tender and so mild.

It was a night so very long ago
When God sent the baby Jesus
For all to know.
They knew he was the one,
And God had kept his promise.
To the world he gave his Son.

Virginia Henderson

The Poor Rich Man

The poor man heard a song.
"If I were a rich man."
Quickly he replied, "Oh but I am."
Then someone asked, "How can that be?
"You have no wealth that I can see."
Smiling, the poor man answered,
"You may not see my wealth.
"It is not laid up here on earth
"By my family who gave me birth.
"My wealth is laid up by God.
"Somewhere beyond the blue.
"I am just a poor rich man passing through."

Virginia Henderson

Quiet Moments

It was early morning as I watched the sun
Shining through the trees.
The sun was making the dew spark
Like diamonds on the leaves.

It was a sight to behold, for me to see.
It was a moment as if God
Had planned it just for me.

I marveled as I thanked him
For his blessing and his grace.
I praised him, and I thanked him
For my quiet moments in this place.

Virginia Henderson

The Promise

Jesus walked upon the water.
He calmed the raging sea,
Then He made a promise
To come back for you and me.

Jesus healed the sick.
At his command, lame men stood up and walked.
He touched blind eyes, and they could see.
Then he made a promise
To come back for you and me.

Jesus cried out, "It is finished!"
As He hung upon the cross at Calvary.
We can claim his promise.
We can follow him.
He will set us free.
And we know, he will keep his promise.
He is coming back for you and me.

Virginia Henderson

My First Poem

In the Shadows

I saw Jesus; he was standing in the shadows.
I could see him plain as day.
I thought it was a dream,
Then my name I heard him say.

Since then much time has come and gone.
Many years have passed away.
He still lingers in the shadows.
He calls out to me each day.

Each day he still lingers in the shadows.
I invited him to stay.
I feel his presence near to me.
He never went away.

Jesus still lingers in the shadows.
It is in the shadows of my heart.
My Savior gave to me his promise.
He said, "I never will depart."

Virginia Henderson

This poem was the second poem.

Turning Point

In my life, I had a turning point.
It was the dawning of a brand-new day.
It was the day I invited Jesus into my life to stay.

I wanted to shout it from the house tops.
I wanted everyone to hear.
I wanted to tell everyone that came close or near.
It was a turning point.
It was a brand-new day.
The day I invited Jesus into my heart to stay.

I was walking on a brand-new track.
I was so happy, I never looked back.
I read my Bible; I found God's glorious truth.
I read about people I never knew
Like the story of Boaz and Ruth.

I read Genesis and Exodus and learned about
Abraham, Isaac, Jacob, Joseph, and Moses.
Their lives were not beds filled with roses.
The study I had was the beginning of a
New understanding for me.
I had a new outlook on life.
I knew what it meant to be free.

I was told that I must understand Genesis
To know what God was getting ready to do.
I read all the stories; I knew they were true.
In the Old Testament, I found Jesus concealed.
In the New Testament, he is revealed.

It was a turning point for me.
It was the dawning of a brand-new day.
It was the day, I learned the truth.
The day I invited Jesus into my heart to stay.

Virginia Henderson

The Vine

Jesus said, "I am the vine, and you are the branches."
The vine produces the fruit for the wine.
Just like life isn't whole without God's Son the divine.

Just like the trees that produces the branches and leaves,
Trees standing proud and tall,
Providing God's shade for us all.

God is the vine and the anchor.
So cling to the vine, hold on to the anchor.
Live by God's promise.
Never be a doubter like Thomas.
Cling to the vine; remember the promise.

Never forget the anchor,
And take chances.
Just remember the vine,
And that we are the branches.

Virginia Henderson

Great Need

Many times it has been said.
The need is so great
The need for more love,
The love that comes from heaven above.

The need in the world is so great.
The forces of evil, their love is to hate.
How can we overcome that evil force?
We followed God's plan.
He gave us the course.

God loved us so much that he sent his own Son
To die for our sin.
And all he asked was for us
To believe in him.

The need is so great; everywhere there is
Turmoil and hate.
Many nations at war.
And we wonder
What are they fighting for?

To some it's for love, and to some it's to hate.
They choose not to believe.
Many have sealed their own fate.
For them it's too late.
But still the need for God's love is so great.

Virginia Henderson

The Lamb

Jesus is the king of kings.
He is the lamb of God.
He is the mighty great I AM.
Born in a lowly stable in Bethlehem,
He died on an old rugged cross at Calvary.
Many thought it was the end of the story.
Three days later he rose from the grave
In all of his glory.
It was the dawning of a brand-new day.
He is alive!
He sits at the right hand of the Father in heaven above.
And to one and all he still offers his grace and love.
The cross is still, there for, a reminder to me.
Jesus died to set me free.
It was all in God's plan.
He sent Jesus as his sacrificial lamb.

Virginia Henderson

The Message of the Cross

The message of the cross leads home
Where we will never again be alone.
Jesus hung on the cross to set us free.
He died on the cross for you and me.
Lift up your head, open your eyes to see.
Behold the cross that leads us home to be free.

Take no detours, just follow the cross,
And you will never be lost.
Prophecy tells us the age is to end.
Then every knee will bend.
Every tongue confesses that Jesus is Lord.
Sing every day, believe, and pray.
Wherever you go, let everyone know.
The way of the cross leads home.

Virginia Henderson

My Cup

In the twenty-third Psalm, David said, "My cup runneth over."
I am just as sure as God provides the cows with clover,
God will fill our cups to running over.

Look to the cross and remember what Jesus did.
Lift up your cup.
He will fill it up.
Jesus will fill it with love, mercy, and grace.
Just like he did when he died in our place.

I sing the song, "I take my cup. I lift it up.
"I pray you hear my voice."
To my Savior, I sing my praise
As my cup to you I raise.

I fill my cup as I lift it up
My cup is overflowing to my savior.
I sing my praise to you.
I sing my thanks for the promises you made.
They are surely coming true.

Virginia Henderson

Loving God

God is so loving, so merciful, and good.
Can I walk in his ways?
I know that I should.

He stands at the door, and knocks.
He waits to give us his love and grace.
God sent him to die in our place.

He is the Word, so merciful and good.
I will answer the door.
I know that I should.

It is a picture so pleasant and bright.
When God gives us his truth and his light,
The love he gives is so good.
I will walk in his ways.
I know that I should.

Jesus said, "Come unto me, you whom are weary."
This was his word, so kind and good.
I am so glad I heard him knock.
I promised him then, in his ways I would walk.

He is so merciful, so loving, and good.
So each day I strive to walk in his ways.
I know that I should.

Virginia Henderson

Our Prayer

Pray that God's glory will dwell in our land.
That God's people will come forth and take a stand.
Pray and ask God to bind us together.
And help us to keep our land free forever.

God will walk us through the valleys,
And some will be like the darkest alleys.
But as long as we walk in God's light,
He will help us to see
When we stand up for what's right.

We must fight for our freedom, liberty, and justice for all.
We need to make sure
What our forefathers gave us won't fall.
But what will remain is sweet liberty
With freedom and justice for all.

Our forefathers gave us a Constitution so great.
It is a God-given document they did create.
It was given to help us live free
In our homeland of sweet liberty.

Virginia Henderson

Take Heart

Take heart and don't despair.
Call upon the Lord
For he does care.

He will walk you through the valleys.
He will meet you on the mountaintops.
His love for you will never ever stop.

The Lord, he keeps his promises.
He gave us many, you see.
He truly came to set us free.
And when he was rejected,
He didn't make one plea.

He just finished the work his Father sent him to do.
He died on the old rugged cross
For me and for you.

So don't despair, take heart.
He is coming, you see.
He keeps his promises.
And we will be free
To live forever with him in eternity.

Virginia Henderson

My Blessing

Jesus gave me his blessing, you see,
When he died on a cross made from a tree.
God watched as his Son paid a great price
For sinners like me.

He gave a great blessing I could receive.
All he asked was for me to believe.
The sweet Holy Spirit oversees all,
Like a refreshing wind,
Reaching out with a whispering call.

Jesus invites us to come to the cross
Where our burdens we can lay down.
Take up your cross,
And one day God will give you a crown.

When I do what Jesus has said, "Only believe."
His blessings I know I will receive.

Virginia Henderson

The Shining Lamp

We cannot shine if we haven't taken time.
Taken time to fill our lamps.
We need God's light in our camps.

Fill each lamp with joy, peace, and love,
Giving us light from the father above.
He is the light of life,
Wiping away the tears
From a world filled with strife.

His word tells me that he is the way,
The truth and the light.
So fill your lamp,
And let it shine bright.

Jesus is our hope.
He is the corner stone of our camp.
So let your light shine forth
And lift up your lamp.

Lift your lamp up for all to see.
Show the light
That sets men free.

Virginia Henderson

God's Touch

To what comfort we do receive
When the Word of God opens our heart,
And we first believe.
We seek the truth.
We seek his face.
We feel the touch of his sweet embrace.

God gave his peace, his word, and grace.
He gave Jesus to die in our place.
Some may believe it's not true.
I pray that's not the course for you.
For me I choose the word, and believe.
And God's blessings, I know I will receive.

Our faith in God is more precious than silver or gold.
Look to the cross.
Stand up, be brave, and be bold.
Then you will shine
Brighter than silver or gold.

Come out from among them,
And let your light shine.
Then God will smile on you and say,
"See! That is a child of mine."

Virginia Henderson

Peace in the Seasons

Spring has arrived, bringing new life
To the hills all around.
God's peace in this place does truly abound.
God gives me a peace in this place
Just as he gives his love and grace.

The hills are majestic in summertime.
Then comes the wonderful beauty of fall,
When the leaves reach their prime
In colors that are simply divine.

Then in God's own timing,
The hills will turn barren and brown.
And soon we can look for the hills
To turn white with snow coming down.

I look at the green hills, and I know it's for a season.
The God I know has his own reason.
For God said in his Word,
"As long as there is a seed, time, and harvest,
There will be a new season."

It is all in God's plan.
He created each season.
He created it all!
And he promised his peace he will give,
If only for him we will live.

Virginia Henderson

Blessed Reservation

I wanted to plan my trip to heaven.
I called to make a reservation.
I was greatly blessed when Jesus answered.
We had quite a conversation.

He asked me, "How can I help you?"
I answered, "I need a ticket to my home in heaven,
And how much is the fare?"
Jesus laughed and said, "Your tickets, it is free if you are going there."

Then Jesus asked, "Do you believe in him who sent me?"
I answered very quickly, "Yes, I do."
Jesus answered, "Your reservations has been made for you, and your
Ticket, it is free."
Then he said, "I stamped it, paid in full at Calvary."

So please call and make your reservation
Have that blessed conversation.
Everything is free.
Jesus paid it all that day at Calvary.
He paid for you, and he paid for me.
He has the tickets,
And they are free.

Virginia Henderson

28

Christmas

Christmas is about a star-filled night.
A night so very long ago.
It was the night Jesus was born
In a stable so low.
As the shepherds watched the stars all aglow,
They didn't think about bright shining trees.
They just whispered, "God, help us, please."

Christmas is coming, it's very near.
Everyone's saying, "It soon will be here."
The carolers are singing. Salvation army pots ringing.
People busy trimming their bright, shining trees.
Silently we whisper, "God, help us, please."

There is shopping to do.
Stores crowded, just like a zoo.
Candies to make. Cookies to bake.
To our friends we will take.
We stop and we look at the bright shining trees.
Then silently whisper, "God, help us, please."

Christmas has come, and the chores are all done.
We stop and we pray to thank God for his Son.
We must remember to pray for this special day.
Christmas has come, and we look at the bright, shining trees.
And silently whisper, "Thank you, God,
"And help us, please."

Virginia Henderson

In Our Place

Jesus promised to leave us his peace.
He said, "My peace I leave with you."
He left us his peace and grace.
Then he died on the cross in our place.

Jesus went to be with his Father in heaven.
He is seated at the Father's right side
Where in this day he still does abide.

He promised that one day he would return.
He gave us his Word and his grace.
He gave it to us when he died in our place.

Look up, give thanks to God above.
Give thanks to him for his love.
Thank him for Jesus, his love, and grace.
Thank him for Jesus who died in our place.

Virginia Henderson

Shepherd Boy and King

David was a little shepherd boy.
Chosen by God to be a king.
David faced a mighty giant.
His weapon was a tiny sling.

The giant Goliath laughed at him and shouted,
"I am not a dog, you puny little thing.
"Come forth, and try to take me with your sling."
David stepped forth and cried, "You come at me
"With dagger, spear, and sword.
"I come at you in the name of the God of hosts
Who is my Lord."

Now David slew the giant big and bold.
Goliath viewed David as a puny little thing
With a harmless little sling.
But God saw David as a king.

Many times this story has been told.
How David slew the giant with a tiny sling,
How David lived to become a mighty warrior,
And to Israel a prophetic king.

Virginia Henderson

Memorial Day

So many answered the call.
To keep America free for you and me.
So we can sing "Sweet Land of Liberty"
Home of the brave and land of the free.

On Memorial Day, let us stop and pray
For so many brave souls.
And we can still say, "Thank you, Lord
"For showing us the way."

Old glory still flies over the land of the free
And the home of the brave.
Off into foreign lands many still go.
Our freedom to save.

Today let us stop and recall.
The season and grief so many have known.
They have kept us free.
And the love of our great country shown.

So on this day I humbly pray.
Thank you, Lord, for this day.
And for your way.
And for all the brave souls, who down through
The years have answered the call.
I say, "God bless them, and thank you all."

Virginia Henderson

Hope

When my eyes are bright with tears,
Still my heart is filled with hope.
I know the Lord is standing near,
Helping me to cope.

I can see him in the sunshine.
I can see him in the rain.
He is always there,
Even in my pain.

I stand upon his Word
That speaks of joy and love.
It is the joy of grace.
He brought from heaven above.

All he asked of me is that I believe.
He asked, "Do you believe in him who sent me?"
I answered, "Yes, I do."
Then I told him that I read it in God's Word
And I know it's true.

Virginia Henderson

The Robe

There is a robe that has no flaws.
It is the robe of righteousness.
It is a robe of perfection.
It was given by Jesus
At his resurrection.

They gambled for his robe at Calvary.
Right at the foot of the cross.
Not one of them realized, what they had done,
Or what they had lost.

His robe of righteousness.
He gave so free a robe without any flaws,
He gave it to sinners like me.
He gave it so we could be free.

Put on the robe of righteousness.
A robe free of flaws and imperfections.
Take up your cross.
Praise God and remember the resurrection.

Virginia Henderson

Footprints

I was walking on the beach counting footprints in the sand.
I knew God was walking with me, He was holding tightly to my hand.
When I looked up, He was smiling down at me.
Then, I watched Him gazing out upon a deep blue sea.
It was a sea of up raised hands praising God, and counting footprints in the sand.
Then, I heard His voice so wonderful and so clear, "Hold fast to me I am always near."
It was then, I felt the sting of hot tears in my eyes, and warm upon my face.
I knew right then, a joy and peace that no one in this world could replace.

Virginia Henderson

First Easter Morn

On the first Easter morn,
Mary hurried to the tomb.
Mary was suffering unbearable grief.
She stumbled along in the dark.
The sun had yet to rise.
Mary could feel the sting,
Of hot tears in her eyes.

Soon Peter arrived, and Mary cried out,
"The stone has been rolled away!"
They found the tomb empty.
What could they say?

Peter turned and fled from the tomb,
Leaving Mary alone.
But not for long.
Soon the angels appeared.
They spoke to Mary with voices soft and clear.

The angel asked Mary, "Why do you seek the
Living amongst the dead?"
Mary was preparing to leave when she heard
Another voice right out of the blue.
It was a voice Mary so readily knew.
Mary cried out, "Master, it is you!"

After speaking with Jesus, Mary went on her way.
The sun was now shining!
It was a new day!
Jesus was alive!
Mary's eyes were no longer stinging with tears.
Mary had a glorious message.
A message that would be passed
down through the years.
Jesus is alive!
He lives!
He never went away.
He lives in our hearts today.

Noah

Noah was a man that found favor with God.
God talked with Noah.
God said, "Noah, I want you to build an ark.
"I will give you the plan."
God said, "Noah, I know you can."

As Noah was working on God's plan,
And building the ark,
The people gathered around and laughed.
To them it was such a lark.

Now Noah worked and stayed obedient to God.
Noah endured, and persevered until he
Finished the ark.
When Noah looked up,
He saw the sky turning dark.

God said, "Noah, close the door!"
Then it started to rain.
Now the people that laughed,
They were all lost in their pain.
Noah had stood on God's promise.
He made it his claim.
God promised Noah dry land.
Noah was sure that the sunshine would follow the rain.

Virginia Henderson

Giving Thanks

On this beautiful Thanksgiving Day.
We bow our heads and we pray.
We give thanks to the Lord above.
We thank him for his many blessings and love.

We give him thanks for the brave ones that choose
Their country so faithfully to serve.
All our thanks to them,
Which they so richly deserve.
Separated from their loved ones
And so many miles away,
When asked why they serve,
"In honor of my country," they say.

We thank God for these brave ones,
And for our great country.
So we give special thanks this day.
It's with thankful hearts
We bow our heads and pray.

We pray for our loved ones
That are absent from us
And can't be here.
We give thanks for our loved ones.
So very dear.
We give special thanks to God above
For watching over us with his special love.

Virginia Henderson

God's Gift

In the little town of Bethlehem,
It was a starry silent night.
The shepherds watched their flocks
And saw a star so very, very bright.

Suddenly their quiet silent night
Had them filled with great fear.
Then the angel appeared within their midst
And stood so very, very near.

The angel said, "Fear not, I bring you
"A message of great joy.
"For you in the city of David,
"This night is born the Savior
"A precious baby boy."

The shepherds quaked! The angels sang.
He is the Son of God!
He is the Son of man!
He is a bright and shining light.
He is the Savior.
He is God's gift to you on this
Beautiful God-given silent night.

Virginia Henderson

A Guiding Light

Jesus is the lighthouse.
He is like the beacon light that searches
For the lost ships at sea.
On broken lives, he shines his light
And sets men free.

Jesus is the beacon light
In the darkest night.
Always a lighthouse
Shining ever bright
In the darkest hour
When hearts are filled with fear.
Jesus is the lighthouse
Always standing near.

Look up and see the lighthouse.
It is there forevermore,
Even in the ship-wrecked lives.
Jesus is the lighthouse.
He will guide us safely to the shore.

Jesus is the lighthouse that will safely guide you
Wherever you may roam.
He is the beacon that keeps on shining
To see you safely home.

Virginia Henderson

Printed in the United States
by Baker & Taylor Publisher Services